SILVER MORNING

Susan Pearson

ILLUSTRATED BY David Christiana

Harcourt Brace & Company

San Diego   New York   London

Text copyright © 1998 by Susan Pearson
Illustrations copyright © 1998 by David Christiana

Requests for permission to make copies of any part of the work should be mailed to:
Permissions Department, Harcourt Brace & Company, 6277 Sea Harbor Drive,
Orlando, Florida 32887-6777.

Library of Congress Cataloging-in-Publication Data
Pearson, Susan.
Silver morning/Susan Pearson; illustrated by David Christiana.
p. cm.
Summary: While waiting for deer to appear, two nature watchers enjoy the beauty
of a foggy silver morning in the woods.
ISBN 0-15-274786-9
[1. Nature—Fiction. 2. Morning—Fiction.]
I. Christiana, David, ill. II. Title.
PZ7.P323316Si 1998
[Fic]—dc21 96-51579

First edition
F E D C B A

Printed in Singapore

The illustrations in this book were done in watercolors on Arches Hot Press Watercolor Paper.
The display type was set in Markus Roman.
The text type was set in Minister Light.
Color separations by Chroma Vision Colour Separation Pte Ltd
Printed and bound by Tien Wah Press, Singapore
This book was printed on totally chlorine-free Nymolla Matte Art paper.
Production supervision by Stanley Redfern and Ginger Boyer
Designed by Lydia D'moch

For Evan, Sara, and Dylan
with love
—S. P.

For Lawrence G.
—D. C.

While we slept . . .

. . . the fog crept in.

When we wake, we cannot see
the road or the mailbox or even the
woodpile. Just bare branches, a patch
of gold that is the field beyond, and a
shadow of distant trees. Everything
else is silver.

We zip our jackets and slip outside, feeling thick with magic. Through the bushes we creep, where tiny drops of water cling to branches like Christmas tree lights.

Then into our February field. Its mushy winter leaves are soft beneath our feet. Its winter grass hides spots of green. Broken limbs, knocked down by last week's storm, lie in its lap like antlers.

We hear a car along the road,
but see only its headlights, like fuzzy
distant eyes. Even its motor sounds
muffled in the fog. A crow caws
straight above us; a lone goose honks;
drops of water from the trees splatter
on the ground.

Quietly we climb the hill, then
down again toward the foggy wall that
is the woods. A rustle in the distance
stops us. Deer! We cannot see them,
but we know that they are here. Their
droppings are like small mounds of
black marbles all around us.

At the old train trestle, we stop and smile and squeeze each other's hands. Carved into its rotting wood in giant letters is LIONEL. It makes us feel like dolls, this giant LIONEL—like little live dolls, tiny figures in a train-set world.

Suddenly the foggy world is busy busy. Squirrels play tag through the trees. One loses its balance and thuds to the ground; we laugh inside, but not aloud, to see it. Crows argue all around us. A chipmunk scurries down the trestle bank, then speeds into its hole near the roots of a crooked tree. We see that hole so clearly, but when we blink, it almost disappears. Creeping closer—quiet quiet—we peek into the tunnel and wish that we were *really* dolls so we could run inside and see our chipmunk's home.

Beyond the trestle, the woods begin. Water drops echo beneath the ancient tracks, and the fog is like a curtain. We peer ahead into the tangled brush. Tangletown, we call it, where vines thicker than our arms twist like snakes along the ground, and thorny thickets grab our legs. We follow deer paths, twisting twisting through the brush. Here and there are worn spots, where deer have slept beside the path. How do they sleep on a bed of thorns?

And then, again, we hear them, racing through the forest up ahead. We see their white tails flash—bright even in the fog—and then no more.

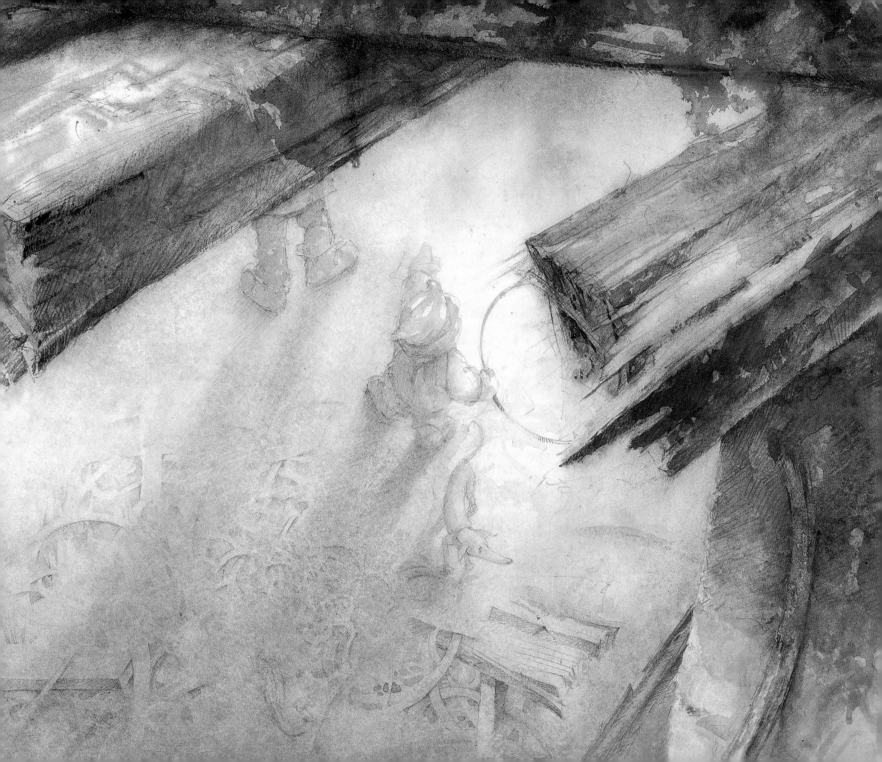

At last we reach the fallen tree. Today we do not ride it, or walk it, or balance on its limbs. Instead we climb right over and leave the brush behind. Before us are the pines. We cannot see their tops today; the fog comes down too low. But we love the needle rug that they have laid beneath our feet. It makes our footsteps velvet, like the fog.

Silently silently we pass through the pines and come to an ancient stone wall. It's hardly a wall at all anymore, it is so crumbling. But even though the wall is old, the woods are older. Why, we wonder, did someone one time build a wall right through the woods?

And now we sit, as still as the stones under us, and wait and watch and wait some more. We look through the trees and hope. Our deer are in there somewhere. Will they feel they're safe again if we are quiet like the fog? Will they let us see them whole, not just their tails?

We sit and sit, for a hundred minutes at least, even though our seats are very cold. But our deer do not come back. The crows are not afraid of us—they scream to let us know. The squirrels don't run and hide. Even timid chipmunks begin to forget that we are here.

But deer are different. Deer are shy. Deer, we think, are like the fog.

Our tummies start to rumble—we left the house before breakfast. We'll see the deer another day; right now, it's time to go home.

We take the easy path, not the one through Tangletown. And we tromp tromp tromp, not caring how much noise we make. We have been quiet long enough. Back over the hill and through the field we march, our thoughts filled with muffins and jam and steaming cups of cocoa.

Suddenly we notice: The fog has lifted. The world's not silver anymore, just as we're not silent. When did it happen? we ask each other. When did the fog disappear?

The fog is even shier than the deer. It crept away so softly, we never saw its white tail flash good-bye.